**W9-BFD-892**

## ABOUT THE BANK STREET READY-TO-READ SERIES

Seventy years of educational research and innovative teaching have given the Bank Street College of Education the reputation as America's most trusted name in early childhood education.

Because no two children are exactly alike in their development, we have designed the *Bank Street Ready-to-Read* series in three levels to accommodate the individual stages of reading readiness of children ages four through eight.

- ○ *Level 1:* GETTING READY TO READ—read-alouds for children who are taking their first steps toward reading.
- ● *Level 2:* READING TOGETHER—for children who are just beginning to read by themselves but may need a little help.
- ○ *Level 3:* I CAN READ IT MYSELF—for children who can read independently.

Our three levels make it easy to select the books most appropriate for a child's development and enable him or her to grow with the series step by step. The *Bank Street Ready-to-Read* books also overlap and reinforce each other, further encouraging the reading process.

We feel that making reading fun and enjoyable is the single most important thing that you can do to help children become good readers. And we hope you'll be a part of Bank Street's long tradition of learning through sharing.

The Bank Street College of Education

*For my friend Marvin Gordon*
—B.B.

THE MAGIC BOX
*A Bantam Little Rooster Book*
*Simultaneous paper-over-board and trade paper editions/September 1990*

*Little Rooster is a trademark of Bantam Books,*
*a division of Bantam Doubleday Dell Publishing Group, Inc.*

*Series graphic design by Alex Jay/Studio J*
*Associate Editor: Gillian Bucky*

*Special thanks to James A. Levine, Betsy Gould,*
*Erin B. Gathrid, and Ana Boix.*

*Library of Congress Cataloging-in-Publication Data*

*Brenner, Barbara.*
*The magic box / by Barbara Brenner ;*
*illustrated by Manuel Boix.*
*p. cm. — (Bank Street ready-to-read)*
*"A Byron Preiss book."*
*"A Bantam little rooster book."*
*Summary: A town cut off from modern civilization*
*and technology is drastically changed by*
*a magic box that shows pictures.*
*ISBN 0-553-05896-7. — ISBN 0-553-34926-0 (pbk.)*
*[1. Television—Fiction.] I. Boix, Manuel, ill.*
*II. Title. III. Series.*
*PZ7.B7518Mag    1990*
*[E]—dc20*

*89-18193    CIP    AC*

*Published simultaneously in the United States and Canada*

*Bantam Books are published by Bantam Books, a division of Bantam Doubleday*
*Dell Publishing Group, Inc. Its trademark, consisting of the words "Bantam Books"*
*and the portrayal of a rooster, is Registered in U.S. Patent and Trademark Office*
*and in other countries. Marca Registrada. Bantam Books, 666 Fifth Avenue, New*
*York, New York 10103.*

PRINTED IN THE UNITED STATES OF AMERICA

0  9  8  7  6  5  4  3  2

Bank Street Ready-to-Read™

# The Magic Box

by Barbara Brenner
Illustrated by Manuel Boix

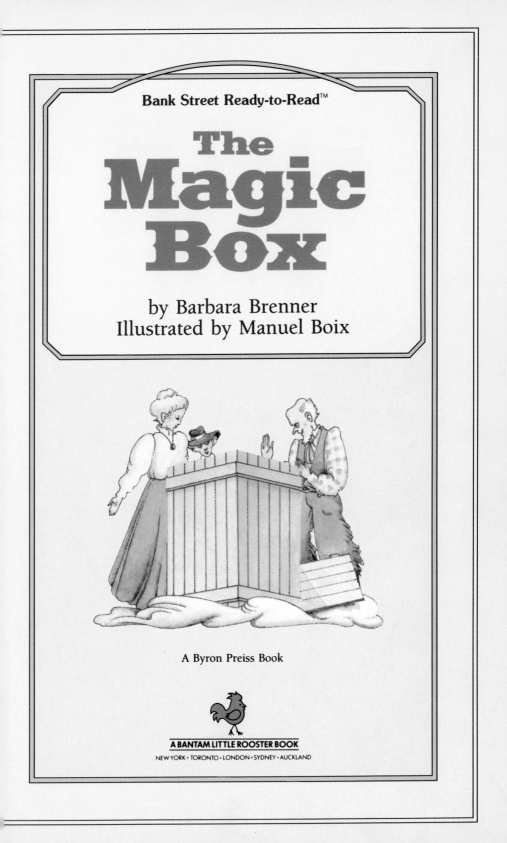

A Byron Preiss Book

A BANTAM LITTLE ROOSTER BOOK

NEW YORK · TORONTO · LONDON · SYDNEY · AUCKLAND

# Chapter 1

There was a town tucked away
in a valley.

It was a busy place.

Travelers came and went.
Peddlers came and went.

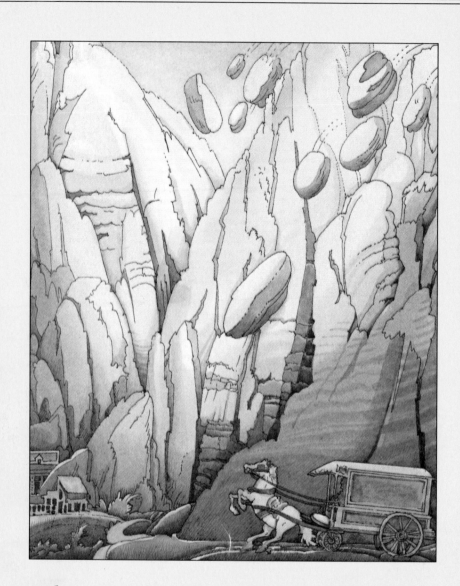

Then one day there was a rock slide.
Rocks as big as houses rolled
into the valley.
They rolled onto the roads
and the train track.

They blocked the little towpaths
that led into town.
Nothing could get out or come in.
The rock slide had cut the town off
from the rest of the world.

9

Years passed.
Grass grew over the old roads
and train track and towpaths.

Things changed outside.
But no travelers or peddlers
came in to tell about the changes.
So folks didn't know about jet planes,
computers, television, and striped
toothpaste

Still, they were happy.
They played ball and read books.
They made quilts and tended their
pole beans and flowers.

They smiled often and didn't seem
to mind that nothing came in
or went out.

Then one day a cargo plane
got lost in a snowstorm.
To save gas, the pilot
ditched a piece of his cargo.
It came sailing out of the sky
and landed in a snowbank
smack in the middle of the town.

## Chapter 2

No one saw the plane.
But everyone saw the box.
Something had come in!
In no time at all everyone was
in the town square.

They stared at the box.
"What can it be?" they asked one
another in hushed voices, as though
the thing inside could hear.

Finally a boy named Marvin
came up with a bright idea.
"Let's open it!" he shouted.

So the mayor got a hammer
and broke open the box.
As the wood fell away,
the crowd grew quiet.

Then someone said,
"It's another box!"
Just then a little girl caught sight
of herself in the screen.

"It's some kind of mirror," she said.
"It's some kind of table," said a man,
putting his bottle of soda pop on it.

"Might be a safe," said another man.
"Maybe you turn those knobs
to open it."
That idea began to catch on.
Then Marvin piped up again.
"It has an electric plug," he said.

They carried the box into the town hall.
The mayor plugged it in.
But nothing happened.
They might have been there all day
if it hadn't been for Marvin.

"Try the knobs," he said.
They did.
First one knob, then another, and
then—MAGIC!

25

They couldn't believe their eyes.
"Do you see what I see?"
they kept asking each other.

26

One child even ran to the back
of the box to see if
the little people were inside it.

That night the mayor called
everyone together.
"Listen, folks," she said.
"This box is clearly a gift
from the outside.

Let's keep our eyes open
and watch it for a message."
Everyone clapped.
Right then and there, they sat down
and started watching.

# Chapter 3

Soon life in the town changed. Each morning people came to watch the box.

They watched cartoons and ads
and game shows.

They watched singing and crying,

eating and shooting.
And they didn't know what
to make of any of it.

But one thing was sure:
the more they watched,
the more they wanted to watch.

Everyone except Marvin.

After a while people began watching
the box all day.
They brought picnic lunches.
The floor got sticky because no one
stopped watching to clean up.

Soon people decided it was silly
to go home to sleep.
So they brought cots
into the town hall.
It was like being at summer camp,
but the floor was stickier.

The box stayed on day and night.
No one played ball or read books.
No one made quilts
or tended their pole beans or flowers.
No one even smiled much.
People wanted to stop watching.
But they were afraid they might
miss the message.

One day the mayor looked around her.
"This town is a mess!" she said.
"Fathers have stopped shaving.
Mothers are wearing bathrobes all day.
Children aren't going to school.
Shopkeepers aren't tending their shops.
And the pole beans are dying!

"I know the box is a gift.
Maybe it *is* magic," she said sadly.
"And maybe it *does* have a message.
But I wish it had never come
into our town at all."

Suddenly, there was Marvin.
He looked up at the mayor.
He looked out at the crowd.
Clearing his throat, he said,
"There is no message for us.

This box is just a machine.
I read about the idea in a book
called *After Radio*."

"You mean it isn't magic?"
asked the mayor.
"Well, it's a *little* magic," Marvin said.
"But a little magic goes a long way."

He went over and turned a knob.
Off went the box.
All the people rubbed their eyes.

It was as though they were waking up from a deep sleep.

After that, people went back
to their old ways.
They played ball and read books.
They made quilts and tended
their pole beans and flowers.

But when they wanted a bit
of the outside to come in,
they would turn on the box.

And, just as Marvin said,
it was a *little* magic.

Barbara Brenner is the author of more than thirty-five books for children, including *Wagon Wheels,* an ALA Notable Book. She writes frequently on subjects related to parenting and is coauthor of *Choosing Books for Kids* and *Raising a Confident Child* in addition to being a senior editor for the Bank Street College Media Group. Ms. Brenner and her husband, illustrator Fred Brenner, have two sons. They live by a lake in Lords Valley, Pennsylvania.

Born and educated in Valencia, Spain, Manuel Boix has illustrated more than twenty books for children and adults, most of which have been published internationally. He has received numerous awards for his work, including Czechoslovakia's Golden Apple and Spain's National Prize for the Best Book for Children. Mr. Boix now lives with his wife and two bilingual children in New York City. Although *The Magic Box* is only his second children's book for an American audience, it's his second with magic in the title. The first was *The Magic Well.*